Ten Little Babies

ROSE IMPEY

Illustrated by
NICOLA SMEE

BLOOMSBURY

LONDON BERLIN NEW YORK SYDNEY

Ten little babies on a sunny day.
Ten little babies left on the grass to play.

And if **one** little baby should start to

crawl away . . .

There'd be **nine** little babies left on the grass to play.

Nine little babies on a sunny day.
Nine little babies left on the grass to play.

And if ONE little baby should start to

float away . . .

There'd be **eight** little babies left on the grass to play.

Eight little babies on a sunny day.
Eight little babies left on the grass to play.

And if ONE little baby should start to

slide away . . .

There'd be SEVEN little babies left on the grass to play.

Seven little babies on a sunny day.
Seven little babies left on the grass to play.

And if **one** little baby should start to

trot away . . .

There'd be SIX little babies left on the grass to play.

SiX little babies on a sunny day.
SiX little babies left on the grass to play.

And if **ONE** little baby should start to

sail away . . .

There'd be **five** little babies left on the grass to play.

Five little babies on a sunny day.
Five little babies left on the grass to play.

And if **one** little baby should start to

climb away . . .

There'd be **four** little babies left on the grass to play.

Four little babies on a sunny day.
Four little babies left on the grass to play.

And if **one** little baby should start to

zoom away . . .

There'd be three little babies left on the grass to play.

Three little babies on a sunny day.
Three little babies left on the grass to play.

And if ONE little baby should start to

hop away...

There'd be tWO little babies left on the grass to play.

TWO little babies on a sunny day.
TWO little babies left on the grass to play.

And if ONE little baby should start to

fly away . . .

There'd be ONE little baby left on the grass to play.

One little baby on a sunny day.
One little baby left on the grass to play.

And if **one** little baby should start to

hide away...

There'd be NO little babies left on the grass to play.

Ten little babies, where can they all be?
Ten little babies, shall we count and see?

One, two, three, four, five,
six, seven, eight, nine, ten.
Ten little babies collected up again.

Ten little babies, it's time they went to bed.
Ten little babies, little sleepyheads.

If we're very quiet . . . shhhh . . .

and no one makes a peep . . .

There'd be **ten** little babies all in their cots asleep.